Dear Parent:
Your child's love of reading starts here!

Every child learns to read in a different way and at his or her own speed. Some go back and forth between reading levels and read favorite books again and again. Others read through each level in order. You can help your young reader improve and become more confident by encouraging his or her own interests and abilities. From books your child reads with you to the first books he or she reads alone, there are I Can Read Books for every stage of reading:

SHARED READING
Basic language, word repetition, and whimsical illustrations, ideal for sharing with your emergent reader

BEGINNING READING
Short sentences, familiar words, and simple concepts for children eager to read on their own

READING WITH HELP
Engaging stories, longer sentences, and language play for developing readers

READING ALONE
Complex plots, challenging vocabulary, and high-interest topics for the independent reader

ADVANCED READING
Short paragraphs, chapters, and exciting themes for the perfect bridge to chapter books

I Can Read Books have introduced children to the joy of reading since 1957. Featuring award-winning authors and illustrators and a fabulous cast of beloved characters, I Can Read Books set the standard for beginning readers.

A lifetime of discovery begins with the magical words "I Can Read!"

Visit www.icanread.com for information
on enriching your child's reading experience.

I Can Read Book® is a trademark of HarperCollins Publishers.

Beat Bugs: Ticket to Ride

Library of Congress Control Number: 2016949896
ISBN 978-0-06-264069-7

Typography by Brenda E. Angelilli

17 18 19 20 21   LSCC   10 9 8 7 6 5 4 3 2   ❖   First Edition

I Can Read!™

BEGINNING READING 1

beat bugs™

Ticket to Ride

adapted by
Cari Meister
based on a story
written by
Erica Harrison
Beat Bugs
created by
Josh Wakely

HARPER
An Imprint of HarperCollinsPublishers

The Beat Bugs are playing tag when they find an odd item.

"What is it?" asks Buzz.

"A machine for riding on," says Crick.

"Like a carnival ride?"

asks Walter.

That gives Jay an idea.

"We can use it to build

our very own ride!" he says.

They all get to work.

They cannot wait to go on the ride!

Soon the ride is ready.

"It's a stink-powered

Crick-o-Wheel,"

says Crick.

Alex the Stinkbug helps

by making a big stink into a tube.

It makes the ride move!

Everyone cheers!

They all climb on board.

Suddenly, the ride stops.

They wonder why.

"Sorry," says Alex.

He ran out of stink.

He can only make more stink

if he eats more golden leaves.

But the Golden Tree is far away.

Kumi offers to go.

But nobody wants to help her.

They would rather play.

So Kumi decides to go get the
leaves by herself.

Kumi walks for a long time.

Finally she spots the Golden Tree.

She picks lots of leaves.

She cannot wait to ride

with her friends.

15

It is dark when Kumi gets back.

She gets an idea.

They can use the leaves

as tickets for the ride.

"Golden tickets for everyone,"

she says.

In the morning,

Buzz is excited about her ticket.

But she chops it up by accident.

How clumsy of Buzz!

Jay uses his ticket to skate faster,

and he loses it when he slips.

How reckless of Jay!

Crick writes ideas on his.

But he rips it up by mistake.

How careless of Crick!

Walter gets hungry.

He eats his ticket.

How silly of Walter!

Everyone gathers around the ride.

"Have your tickets ready,"

says Kumi.

But no one has a ticket anymore!

Only Kumi has a ticket to ride.

She has to ride alone.

The Beat Bugs are mad at Kumi.

How could she have fun without them?

Jay thinks she does not care

about them.

Kumi is hurt by her friends.

"I do care!" says Kumi.

"I wanted us all to ride together.

That would have been more fun."

The Beat Bugs have let Kumi down.

First they did not help her.

Then they lost their tickets.

Now Kumi is upset.

"We have to do something!" says Jay.

Jay, Crick, Buzz, and Walter

go off to the Golden Tree.

They gather more leaves.

Walter gets hungry.

He wants to eat the leaves.

But the Beat Bugs stop him

just in time.

When they get back,

they show Kumi the tickets they got.

Now everyone can go on the ride!

Kumi is happy to have friends

like the Beat Bugs.

That night, all of the Beat Bugs have fun on the ride—together.

"Ticket to Ride" lyrics

Written by John Lennon/Paul McCartney

I think I'm gonna be sad, I think it's
    today, yeah!
The girl that's driving me mad is
    going away.

She's got a ticket to ride, she's got
    a ticket to ride.
She's got a ticket to ride,
    and she don't care.

She's got a ticket to ride, she's got
    a ticket to ride.
She's got a ticket to ride,
    and she don't care.

I don't know why she's riding
    so high.
She ought to think twice,
    she ought to do right by me
Before she gets to saying goodbye,
She ought to think twice,
    she ought to do right by me

I think I'm gonna be sad, I think it's
    today, yeah!
The girl that's driving me mad is
    going away.

She's got a ticket to ride, she's got
    a ticket to ride.
She's got a ticket to ride,
    and she don't care.

I don't know why she's riding
    so high.
She ought to think twice,
    she ought to do right by me
Before she gets to saying goodbye,
She ought to think twice,
    she ought to do right by me

She's got a ticket to ride, she's got
    a ticket to ride.
She's got a ticket to ride, and
    she don't care.

My baby don't care
My baby don't care
My baby don't care
My baby don't care
My baby don't care
My baby don't care